Who's Got A NORMAL Family?

B.N. For Max, Frances and Scott.

M.A. For Babi, my husband and my children.

First published in Australia in 2016
by Little Steps Publishing
48 Ross St
Glebe NSW 2037
www.littlesteps.com.au

National Library of Australia Cataloguing-in-Publication entry
Creator: Nowell, Belinda, author. Title: Who's Got a Normal Family?
/ written by Belinda Nowell ; illustrated by Miša Alexander.

ISBN: 9781925117752 (hardback)

Other Creators/Contributors: Alexander, Miša, illustrator.

Dewey Number: A8234
Printed in China

Designed by Angel Rae McMullan

Who's Got A NORMAL Family?

Belinda Nowell

Illustrated by Miša Alexander

It was News Day in Alex's class and today he had
something extra special to tell everyone.

'I have a new baby sister called Emma.'
Alex explained Baby Emma hadn't come from his mummy's tummy.

Baby Emma was almost one and had arrived last night, while Alex was eating macaroni and meatballs. Baby Emma was his brand new foster sister.

All the kids clapped. Well, most of them.
Not Jimmy Martin. 'Babies are boring!' he yelled.

Jimmy Martin had a stomp in his step and an upside-down smile.

He did not like anyone to be happy.

Suddenly Alex wasn't so excited anymore because,

just like Baby Emma,
Alex was a foster child too.

Alex was normally the sort of boy who laughed his way from breakfast to dinner,

but that afternoon he did not laugh at all.
He even cried behind his hands when he thought no one was watching.

That night, Alex's mummy gave him an extra-squeezy hug
but he was still worried. 'Are we normal?' he asked.

Mummy gave Alex her brightest smile.
'Absolutely NOT ... but why don't we find out who is?'

Together they searched Alex's class
photo for a kid with a normal family.

Katie was very good at climbing trees … but always got stuck at the top.
Her grandmother had to climb up every time to rescue her.

'Katie lives with her grandmother,'
said Alex. 'That's not normal.'

Alir's family moved here because their home was no longer safe. Alir never misses a shot at goal — he's that good. Everyone wants to be on his football team.

'But Alir lives with his grandma, aunty, two uncles AND
his cousins too,' said Alex. 'That's not normal.'

Eva ::: **Riley** :::

Eva loved dressing up and won the book week costume competition every year. She was always going camping too.

'Eva's daddy is so funny,' said Alex.
'But she doesn't have a mummy. That's not normal.'

Tim had a collection of goggles and was the only kid who liked getting his face wet.
'He can stay underwater for a very long time,' said Alex.

'That can't be normal. And he's adopted,
so that's a double un-normal.'

HENRY

HALE - GARCIA

Henry had extra-fast sports shoes and threw the best parties.
He even had his own birthday fireworks.

'But Henry has two daddies
and no mummy,' said Alex.
'That's not normal.'

Samantha lived around the corner in a big house with a bus as a family car.

'Samantha was normal,' said Alex, 'but then Samantha's mum
married Nathan's dad and now she has five new brothers.'

Soon there was only one kid left.
Jimmy Martin.

But Alex's mummy thought his family was different too. She wondered if Jimmy was sad because his daddy didn't live with him anymore.

Alex thought they'd never find a normal family.

That night, after an extra story and goodnight song, Mummy
whispered something in Alex's ear that made him smile.

The next day, Alex was happy again but he thought he saw
Jimmy Martin crying behind his hands.

Alex showed him where the best lizards lived and told him
what his mummy had said.

'All families are different, and that's the most normal thing of all.'